Something Good

Something Good

STORY by
ROBERT MUNSCH

ART by
MICHAEL MARTCHENKO

annick press
toronto • berkeley

© 2018 Bob Munsch Enterprises Ltd. (text)
© 2018 Michael Martchenko (illustrations)
Designed by Emma Dolan (2018)
Second printing, June 2019

Original publication:
© 1990 Bob Munsch Enterprises Ltd. (original text)
© 1990 Michael Martchenko (illustrations)

We acknowledge the support of the Canada Council for the Arts and the Ontario Arts Council, and the participation of the Government of Canada/la participation du gouvernement du Canada for our publishing activities.

Library and Archives Canada Cataloguing in Publication

Munsch, Robert N., 1945-, author
    Something good / Robert Munsch ; [illustrations by] Michael Martchenko.

(Classic Munsch)
Previously published: Toronto : Annick Press, 1990.
ISBN 978-1-77321-087-2 (hardcover).--ISBN 978-1-77321-086-5 (softcover)

    I. Martchenko, Michael, illustrator II. Title.

PS8576.U575S6 2018   jC813'.54   C2018-901424-5

Published in the U.S.A. by Annick Press (U.S.) Ltd.
Distributed in Canada by University of Toronto Press.
Distributed in the U.S.A. by Publishers Group West.

Printed in China

www.annickpress.com
www.robertmunsch.com

Also available in e-book format. Please visit www.annickpress.com/ebooks.html for more details.

To Tyya, Andrew,
Julie, and Ann Munsch
Guelph, Ontario

Tyya went shopping with her father and her brother and her sister. She pushed the cart up the aisle and down the aisle, up the aisle and down the aisle, up the aisle and down the aisle.

Tyya said, "Sometimes my father doesn't buy good food. He gets bread, eggs, milk, cheese, spinach—nothing any good! He doesn't buy

ICE CREAM!
COOKIES!
CHOCOLATE BARS!
or GINGER ALE!"

So Tyya very quietly snuck away from her father and got a cart of her own. She pushed it over to the ice cream. Then she put one hundred boxes of ice cream into her cart.

Tyya pushed that cart up behind her father and said, "DADDY, LOOK!"

Her father turned around and yelled, "YIKES!"

Tyya said, "DADDY! GOOD FOOD!"

"Oh, no," said her father. "This is sugary junk. It will rot your teeth. It will lower your IQ. Put it ALL BACK!"

So Tyya put back the one hundred boxes of ice cream. She meant to go right back to her father, but on the way she had to pass the candy. She put three hundred chocolate bars into her cart.

Tyya pushed that cart up behind her father and said, "DADDY, LOOK!"

Her father turned around and said, "YIKES!"

Tyya said, "DADDY! GOOD FOOD!"

"Oh, no," said her father. "This is sugary junk. Put it **ALL BACK!**"

So Tyya put back all the chocolate bars.

Then her father said, "Okay, Tyya, I have had it. You stand here and **DON'T MOVE.**"

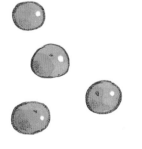

Tyya knew she was in BIG trouble, so she stood there and DIDN'T MOVE.

Some friends came by and said hello. Tyya didn't move.

A man ran over her toe with his cart. Tyya still didn't move.

A lady who worked at the store came by and looked at Tyya. She looked her over from the top down, and she looked her over from the bottom up. She knocked Tyya on the head—and Tyya still didn't move.

The lady said, "This is the nicest doll I have ever seen. It looks almost real." She put a price tag on Tyya's nose that said $29.95. Then she picked Tyya up and put her on the shelf with all the other dolls.

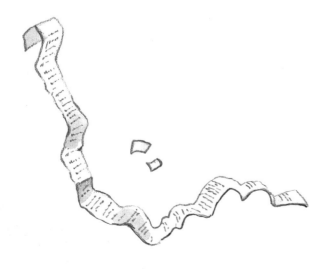

A man came along and looked at Tyya. He said, "This is the nicest doll I have ever seen. I'm going to get that doll for my son." He picked up Tyya by the hair.

Tyya yelled, very loudly, "STOP."

The man screamed, "EYAAAAH! IT'S ALIVE!" And he ran down the aisle, knocking over a pile of five hundred apples.

A lady came along and looked at Tyya. She said,
"This is the nicest doll I have ever seen. I think I will buy
this doll for my daughter." She picked up Tyya by the ear.

Tyya yelled, as loudly as she could, "STOP."

The lady screamed,
"EYAAAAH! IT'S ALIVE!"

And she ran down the aisle,
knocking over a pile of
five hundred oranges.

Then Tyya's father came along, looking for his daughter. He said, "Tyya? Tyya? Tyya? Tyya? Where are you? . . . **TYYA!** What are you doing on that shelf?"

Tyya said, "It's all your fault. You told me not to move and people are trying to buy me, **WAAAAAHHHHH!**"

"Oh, come now," said her father. "I won't let anybody buy you." He gave Tyya a big kiss and a big hug; then they went to pay for all the food.

The man at the cash register looked at Tyya and said, "Hey, Mister, you can't take that kid out of the store. You have to pay for her. It says so right on her nose: twenty-nine ninety-five."

"Wait," said the father. "This is my own kid. I don't have to pay for my own kid."

The man said, "If it has a price tag, you have to pay for it."

"I won't pay," said the father.

"You've got to," said the man.

The father said, "NNNNO."

The man said, "YYYYES."

The father said, "NNNNO!"

The man said, "YYYYES!"

The father and Andrew and Julie all yelled, "NNNNNNO!"

Then Tyya quietly said, "Daddy, don't you think I'm worth twenty-nine ninety-five?"

"Ah . . . Um . . . I mean . . . Well, of course you're worth twenty-nine ninety-five," said the father. He reached into his wallet, got out the money, paid the man, and took the price tag off Tyya's nose.

Tyya gave her father a big kiss, SMMMERCCHH, and a big hug, MMMMMMMMMM, and then she said, "Daddy, you finally bought something good after all."

Then her father picked up Tyya and gave her a big long hug—and didn't say anything at all.